The Big Tree Gang

Jo Ellen Bogart

with illustrations by
Dean Griffiths

ORCA BOOK PUBLISHERS

Library and Archives Canada Cataloguing in Publication

Bogart, Jo Ellen, 1945-
The big tree gang / Jo Ellen Bogart; with illustrations by Dean Griffiths.
(Orca echoes)

ISBN 10: 1-55143-345-1 / ISBN 13: 978-1-55143-345-5

I. Griffiths, Dean, 1967- . II. Title. III. Series.
PS8553.O465B53 2005   JC813'.54   C2005-904061-0

First Published in the United States, 2005
Library of Congress Control Number: 2005929690

Summary: A pair of twins and their two best friends have a series of adventures
together in their small woodland town.

*Orca Book Publishers is dedicated to preserving the environment and has printed this book
on paper certified by the Forest Stewardship Council®.*

Orca Book Publishers gratefully acknowledges the support for its publishing
programs provided by the following agencies: the Government of Canada through the
Canada Book Fund and the Canada Council for the Arts, and the Province of British
Columbia through the BC Arts Council and the Book Publishing Tax Credit.

Design and typesetting by John van der Woude

ORCA BOOK PUBLISHERS
PO Box 5626, Stn. B
Victoria, BC Canada
V8R 6S4

ORCA BOOK PUBLISHERS
PO Box 468
Custer, WA USA
98240-0468

www.orcabook.com
Printed and bound in Canada.

14 13 12 11 • 5 4 3 2

To nature-loving children everywhere.

The Bug Walk

It was a beautiful Saturday morning. Sitting at the breakfast table, Keely saw a butterfly flutter past the kitchen window.

"Hey," she said to her brother, Reg. "This is a good day for a bug walk!"

"What is it with you and bugs?" he asked. "Rocks are so much better."

Keely got a serious look on her face and started to sing,

> Rocks are boring, rocks are dead.
> Reg has rocks in his head.

"Rocks don't do anything," Keely said with a sniff.

"That's why I like them," Reg said. "They don't fly away, they don't bite and they last a long time."

Keely used the butter knife to paint a butterfly shape on her toast with blueberry jam.

"Mom, Keely got butter in the jam jar," said Reg.

"Look, Mom," Keely said, holding up the butterfly.

"Lovely, Keely," said her mother. "How about some strawberry spots?"

"Yum," said Keely, reaching for the strawberry jam.

"Gorgeous," said Keely's mother when she saw the finished butterfly.

"Delicious," said Keely as she nibbled at the edges.

"That kind of bug I like," said Reg. He chomped a bite out of one wing as Keely tried to snatch it out of his reach. Reg wiped jam off his mouth and looked at his watch. "Time to meet Shawna and Burt," he said.

Keely and Reg headed off toward the huge hollow oak they called Big Tree. Every day they met their best friends, Shawna and Burt, at Big Tree. Keely saw a praying mantis on the path and picked it up. It was just a small one. It perched on her finger with its elbows bent.

"You're a cutie," she said and put it on her head.

"Good grief," said Reg.

"I'll call you Fred," Keely said to the insect. "You can ride up there for a while. You're not afraid of heights, are you, Fred?" Keely started to sing.

Up on my head,
Teeny tiny Fred
Having a ride,
You don't have to hide.

"Sometimes you are so weird, Keely," said Reg.

They went on walking. Keely stopped to look at a stinkbug. Reg watched for interesting rocks for his collection.

When they got to Big Tree, Burt was leaning against its broad trunk, waiting for them.

"Where's Shawna?" Keely asked.

"She's coming soon," Burt said. Then he gasped and screamed. "Ahhhhh! There's a terrible thing on your head!"

"What terrible thing?" she asked.

"Oh, it's awful, green with bulgy eyes and stickery spines on its arms," Burt said, shaking. "Ugh, I can't look."

"Burt!" said Keely. "Calm down! It's just a praying mantis. His name is Fred and he's cute." She held out the insect.

"He's creepy," said Burt. "How can you touch him?"

"Keely likes things with lots of legs," said Reg.

"Burt," Keely said, "bugs are fun, except for the ones that bite and sting. This one doesn't."

"I guess you are going to tell Burt that your mantis wouldn't hurt a fly," said Reg.

"A fly?" said Keely. "Well, no. Fred would eat a fly. But Burt, you are not a fly."

"I feel like a fly when he looks at me," said Burt, shivering.

Reg took Burt by the arm. "Come on, Burt. Let's play jump-the-stump. You'll feel better."

Before they had jumped the stump three times, Shawna came.

"Burt is afraid of bugs," Keely said.

"Thanks for telling everyone," said Burt.

Shawna laughed. "Don't be silly," she told Burt. "We all have things we're afraid of."

"Really?" said Burt. "What are you afraid of?"

"High places," said Shawna. "I don't like being up high."

"I don't mind high places at all," said Burt.

"See what I mean?" said Shawna. "You're not afraid of everything, just some things. Maybe you can get over your fear."

"I have an idea," said Keely. "Let's go for a bug walk. We'll find insects and lots of other little things that creep and crawl. I really like spiders and things with millions of legs."

Burt looked worried. "Um, uh…" he stuttered.

"Let's start by the pond," said Keely. "We can look at the water striders. Come on."

"See how they stay on top of the water?" said Shawna. She pointed to some long-legged bugs.

"They look like they're skating," said Burt.

"Now, look at this spider," Keely called. "He has trapped a little bubble of air under the water to breathe from."

"Like a scuba diver," said Burt, trying to see through the water.

"Here's an ant nest," said Reg. "How do you like ants, Burt?"

"Mine are very nice," said Burt. "So are my uncles."

Shawna giggled at Burt's joke.

"Not aunts, Burt. Ants," said Keely. "Tiny, little, hardworking ants. See them carrying food back to their nest?"

"They're kind of interesting," said Burt. "I don't mind watching them, from over here. I'm feeling a little better."

"Good," said Shawna, "because now it's time to look under rocks."

She reached for a flat rock and turned it over.

"Wow!" Shawna said. "Look at this millipede all curled round and round. Hey, Burt, count the legs on this little guy. Feel how smooth he is."

Burt put his hands behind his back. He shook his head. "Not me!"

Shawna put the millipede down on the ground. Its legs rippled as it tried to get back to a hiding place.

"Too many legs," Burt said, looking a little queasy. Just then, a dragonfly landed on his shoulder. Burt turned his head to look into its big eyes.

"How are you doing there, Burt?" asked Reg.

"Okay," he said. "I'm doing okay. It's not too bad."

"Great!" said Keely. She grinned and wrinkled her nose at Burt. "Before long, you'll be ready…for Fred."

"I think Burt has had enough bugs for today," said Reg. "I'm going to show him some nice, restful rocks."

Burt laughed. "That sounds great, Reg. Bring them on."

Keely's Cold

Keely woke up with a terrible cold.

"Mom!" she called. "I feel awful. I'm hot and cold, my throat hurts and I can't breathe!"

Keely's mom stuck her head through the doorway. "Oh dear," she said. "I thought you might be getting sick when you sneezed last night. I'll get you a nice breakfast to make you feel better."

"No!" said Keely. And in her croaky voice she sang,

> I'm not hungry.
> I'm not thirsty.

I hate everything.

I'll just starve.

"If that's what you want, dear," said Keely's mother.

Keely lay in her bed for a while, grumbling to herself. She heard a funny sound. It was her stomach growling. Then her throat began to feel dry. "Mom," she called.

Keely's mother walked in with a tray. Keely saw a big glass of orange juice, a boiled egg in a yellow eggcup, a buttered scone with Keely's favorite crabapple jelly and a steaming cup of blackberry tea.

"I thought you might change your mind," Keely's mother said.

Keely scrunched one eyebrow way down. She lifted the other one way up. She nibbled at the scone and sipped the juice. Her stomach felt a bit better. She sipped the tea. Her throat felt better. She could even breathe a little.

"That's great, Mom," Keely said. She sighed. "Thanks."

Keely's mother kissed her hot cheek. "You're welcome, Keely," she said.

Just then Reg popped his head around the corner. "Is it safe to come in? Mom said you're sick and not too happy either."

"How can I be happy when I'm sick?" she asked.

"I'll try to take your mind off being sick," said Reg. He made a funny face. Keely groaned. She started to cough.

Two heads popped up outside Keely's open window. Shawna and Burt grinned at Keely. "Are you coming out to play?" they asked.

Keely frowned at them. "I'm sick," she said.

"We can keep you company here," said Burt.

"We can sing to you," said Shawna.

Keely looked away. She started to sing,

I feel awful.
I feel terrible.
I hate everything.
Leave me alone.

"Okay," said Burt. "You can be alone."

Keely looked at the window. Shawna and Burt were gone.

"I guess that leaves me out too," said Reg. He walked out of the room.

Keely tossed and turned. She grumbled. She nibbled her nails and blew her nose. Then she began to feel funny. She did not like how she felt. She felt lonely.

"Hey!" she called.

Two heads popped up outside the window. This time it was Shawna and Reg.

"What?" asked Shawna.

"I need some company," Keely said.

"We'll be right in," said Shawna.

Reg popped into the bedroom. "I thought you'd change your mind," said Reg. "Burt went home for a board game, in case you're bored. Get it? Bored?"

Keely made a face.

"It was Burt's joke," said Reg.

Keely laughed. "I guess I'm kind of awful when I'm sick, aren't I?"

"Awful," said Shawna.

"Horrible," said Reg.

"Terrible," said Burt.

"You're back," said Keely. "What game did you bring?"

"Nuttyland," he said. "And if you'll stop being grumpy, we can all have a good time."

"Right," said Shawna. "We like you all the time, but we like you better when you're not grumpy."

"I like me better not grumpy too...ahhhhh... ahhhhh..." Keely grabbed for a tissue and sneezed. "You guys sit over there, and someone move my marker for me, or else you'll all get sick."

"Okay," said Burt. "Spin the arrow to see who goes first, Shawna."

"Don't you think the sick one should go first?" asked Keely.

"No!" they all said. "Play fair, Keely."

Shawna got to go first. She spun seven and went to the cave. Burt got sent to the river. He found a magic stone. Keely went next. She got as far as the woodland path. Reg spun. He landed on "Lose a turn."

"Too bad," said Keely to Reg.

Later, Shawna found a treasure. Reg lost another turn.

"Too bad for me again," he said.

Then Shawna lost the treasure down a deep hole. Keely got stuck up a tall tree. Reg fell in the river. Burt made it up the mountain and won.

"Great game," said Burt.

"It was a great game," said Shawna, "even if I did come in last."

"You can't beat a good game with good friends," said Reg.

"And you guys are good friends," said Keely. "Come again tomorrow, okay?"

"We will," Burt and Shawna said. They left Keely to get some rest.

That night after supper, Keely's father came in with cough medicine and a book.

Keely swallowed the medicine. "Yuck!" she said.

"Would you like to hear a story?" her father asked.

Keely told her father how grumpy she had been

with her mother and Reg and her friends. "I said I would just starve, but Mom brought me breakfast anyway," she said. "And I told everyone to leave me alone, but they stayed to keep me company anyway."

"That was nice of them," said Keely's father.

Keely smiled. "Just in case you don't know how I really feel," she said to her father, "I feel awful, and I feel horrible, but I really want you here and I really want to hear a story. Thanks, Dad."

Keely's father gave her a hug. "Well, here I am and here is your story." And he opened the book to read.

The Golden Tulip

The wind came up on a spring morning as Reg and Keely were walking to school.

"This looks good," said Reg.

"It sure does," said Keely.

It was still windy at recess. It was windier at lunch and very windy on the walk home.

"This is the day we have been waiting for," said Reg.

"Oh boy!" Keely shouted. "Race you home!"

Keely and Reg got out the kites they had made in the cold days of winter. They had been saving them for a day just like this.

"Oh, how beautiful the butterfly will look aloft," said Keely holding up her kite.

"Aloft?" said Reg.

"Aloft," said Keely. "In the air, in the sky, flying high…"

"Oh no, here comes a poem," said Reg. He laughed.

Keely punched him on the arm.

Reg held up his fish-shaped kite. "Well," he said, "my minnow will swim in the clouds, way above your butterfly."

"We'll see," Keely said. She smiled to herself.

Keely and Reg ran all the way to the big meadow.

"This is the best place," said Reg. "There is lots of room to run. There are no trees to tear the kites."

The strong wind lifted the kites. It pulled the strings through Keely's and Reg's fingers. The kites grew smaller and smaller as they rose in the sky.

Reg said to Keely, "If we get them too high, it will be harder to save them if the wind dies."

"The wind won't die, scaredy-cat," said Keely. "It's been getting stronger all day. You just don't like it that my kite is higher than yours."

"No way," said Reg. "Mine is way higher."

Keely laughed and started singing,

> Reg is a liar
> If he says his kite is higher.

She began to dance around. Just then, her kite stopped pulling on the string.

"Oh no," Reg cried. "The wind is dying down. Reel in your kite! Hurry!"

"I'm winding as fast as I can," Keely shouted. She ran into the wind. "We have to keep them from crashing!"

Reg and Keely ran and ran. They wound the string around the rolls as fast as they could, but the kites were falling fast.

"Oh no!" said Reg. "We are close to Mr. Webber's place. We can't let the kites fall into his garden! Remember how mad he was the last time?"

"I remember," Keely said. "Run faster!"

The kites fluttered back and forth as they fell toward the hedge around Mr. Webber's garden. As Keely and Reg ran, they heard a loud voice yelling.

"Ruined!" the voice cried. Mr. Webber's head appeared over the top of the hedge. "All ruined! Your kites have crushed my prize tulips! Rotten kids! No respect for other people's things!"

"No, no, we never meant…" said Reg.

"We're so sorry," said Keely.

"Go!" said Mr. Webber. He threw the kites over the hedge. "Take your tulip-killing kites and go!"

Keely and Reg picked up their broken kites and started home.

"I've never seen anyone so mad," said Reg, "or so mean."

"Mom says he's just a lonely man with no friends," said Keely.

"Who could be friends with a grouch like that?" Reg said. "Humph!"

"Maybe we could give him something to say we're sorry," Keely said.

When they got home, they told their mother what had happened.

"Too bad," she said. "He wasn't so grumpy when I was your age. And you know, I remember him flying kites with his children, laughing and singing."

"Really?" said Reg. "That's hard to imagine."

"He was young once too," said their mother. "He was even a boy once. Now his kids live far away and never come to visit."

"Wow!" said Reg. "A kid like us. Hmmm. Maybe he still likes kites just a little." He called to his sister, "Keely, I have an idea."

"Wonderful!" said Keely, when he told her his plan. "It's a great idea. Can we make one shaped like a tulip?"

"I think so," said Reg. "You draw the design. I'll get the things we need."

They worked all evening. When it was finished, Reg held up a beautiful yellow tulip-shaped kite. "We'll call it the Golden Tulip," said Keely.

Reg smiled. "And we'll take it over tomorrow."

On the way to Mr. Webber's house the next day, Reg said to Keely, "He might be pretty grumpy."

"I would bet on it," Keely said.

Before they got to Mr. Webber's gate, they heard his voice.

"So, you're back to kill more tulips, are you?" Mr. Webber's eyebrows were pulled down over his eyes as he peered at them over the hedge.

"We brought you this," Keely said. "We are sorry for hurting your flowers."

Mr. Webber stared at the kite. His eyebrows lifted. "For me? It's beautiful. I haven't had a kite in years." He reached out and touched the kite. "But... I could never fly it. These old legs won't go anymore."

"We'll help you," said Keely, "if you want us to."

Mr. Webber's eyes lit up. "Would you do that?" he said.

"Sure," said Reg. "We can go with you to the meadow and try to get the Golden Tulip aloft."

"The Golden Tulip aloft," said Mr. Webber. "Yes, that sounds good! Let's go!"

They walked very slowly with Mr. Webber. The wind in the meadow was gentle but steady. Mr. Webber held the kite high and faced into the wind. His face broke into a huge grin.

"Ready, Mr. Webber?" said Keely.

"Ready!" said Mr. Webber. Keely took off running. The kite lifted from Mr. Webber's hands. He clapped and whistled. "Whoopee!" he yelled.

The Golden Tulip rose quickly.

"She's a beauty!" said Mr. Webber. "Such a beauty."

Keely put the kite string in Mr. Webber's hand. The Golden Tulip moved back and forth in the sky, tugging on the string.

"Oh, this feels so good," said Mr. Webber. "I haven't flown a kite in so long. I feel like a boy again." He moved around on his stiff legs, almost dancing in the short grass. "Whoopee!" he yelled. "Look at me!"

"He likes it," said Reg.

"He loves it," said Keely. "This was one of your best ideas, Reg."

"You kids are okay," Mr. Webber said. "When we're done here, I will make you the best hot chocolate you've ever tasted."

"We love hot chocolate!" Keely and Reg said together.

"And I," said Keely, "would like to see your flowers. I love flowers."

"Wonderful," said Mr. Webber. "And what do you like?" he asked Reg.

"Rocks!" Reg said. "Rocks are nice."

"Then you will like my rock garden," said Mr. Webber. He laughed.

"You know," Reg said to Keely, "I'm glad the wind crashed our kites into Mr. Webber's tulips."

"Me too," said Keely.

Keely and Reg Play Fair

One dreary, drippy, drizzly day, Keely and Reg spent the whole afternoon playing together inside.

They played dress-up by the front windows. They played board games on the rug and raced cars behind the sofa. They worked jigsaw puzzles on the coffee table. They drew funny pictures of their friends. They played records while they sailed tiny boats in the fish tank.

Then their mother came in. "Dinner is in one hour," she said. "I would like you to clean up all of your things by then."

"Yes, Mother," said Reg.

"Okay, Mom," said Keely.

"There's a lot of stuff here," said Keely to her brother. "This is going to be a lot of work."

"I know," said Reg. "And I hope that you do your share."

"I'm sure I see more of your toys here," said Keely, "so you should have more to do."

"Don't be silly," said Reg. "We both played with all the toys, so we both clean up all the toys."

"But what if I work faster and do more?" asked Keely.

"You? Fast?" said Reg. He laughed. "I don't think that will be a problem."

"Hrumph!" said Keely. "I think you want me to do it all!"

Mother stuck her head in. "I know that my two smart kids can figure out a way to share the work fairly." She smiled and went back to the kitchen.

"Okay," said Reg. "How about I do the high stuff and you do the low stuff?"

"There's more low stuff," said Keely.

"Then I do the front part of the room and you do the back," he said.

Keely frowned. "There's more stuff in the back. Besides, where does the front stop and the back begin?"

"I know," said Reg. He went into his room. He came back with a rope. "This will help," he said.

"Are we going to skip rope? I like to skip rope." Keely took the rope and jumped hot peppers.

"No, no, no," said Reg.

"Uncle Randolph showed me how to twirl a rope cowboy-style," Keely said. She swung the rope over her head.

"That's not what it's for," said Reg.

"Oh, I know. Don't tell me. The rope is a snake. We are going to play snake charmer. Right?"

"No, no," said Reg. "I didn't bring the rope for more playing. It is to help us clean up."

Keely put one eyebrow down. She put the other eyebrow up. "The rope will help us clean up?" she said. Then she smiled. "Is it a magic rope? I like magic."

"No," said Reg. "We put the rope down the middle of the room. I clean one side and you clean the other. Understand?"

Keely gave him a look and pointed her finger at him. "You are going to take the easy side for yourself. I know you are."

"No, no. This will be really fair. One of us will put the rope down, and the other one will get to choose which side to clean."

Keely squinted and looked at Reg sideways. "So you can't make an easy side and pick it yourself?" she said.

"That's right," said Reg. "Do you want to put down the rope or get first pick of sides?"

Keely thought. "That's tricky," she said, but at last she reached for the rope. She ran it down the middle of the room.

"Too much on the left," she said and moved the rope. "Too much on the right now. All those little building blocks will take a lot of work."

"So will the puzzle pieces," said Reg.

"You're right," said Keely. She moved the rope again. "This isn't easy," she said. "I should get extra credit for doing the rope."

"Good grief!" said Reg.

"Fifteen minutes until dinner," Mother called.

"Acch!" said Reg.

"Oh dear," said Keely. "That's not enough time to do it all."

"Let's just do it!" said Reg. He scooped up pieces from the jelly-bean jigsaw puzzle and put them in the box.

"What happened to the hour we had?" asked Keely. She packed away the racing cars and boats.

"I guess we spent a lot of time arguing," Reg said as he put the board games in their boxes.

"But the rope part was fun," said Keely.

"Yes, I guess it was," said Reg. He swept up pieces of paper. Keely picked up scissors and glue.

"Wash your hands for dinner," called their mother.

"Made it!" said Keely. She put away the last record.

"We're a good team," said Reg. He slid the last book into the bookshelf.

"A very good team," said Keely.

Busted

"The letter carrier's coming!" Reg called, looking out the window. Keely raced to the door to wait with Reg.

"Is this what you're waiting for?" asked the letter carrier. He handed each of them an envelope.

"It sure is!" said Reg. The twins ripped open their envelopes. Inside each was a crisp bill and a birthday card from their Uncle Randolph.

"Thank you, Uncle Randolph!" said Keely.

"You said it!" said Reg, "Let's go to the store!"

Keely and Reg had already picked out the perfect birthday presents the week before.

"Bye, Mom," they called as they raced out of the house.

"Hi, Mr. Brown," Keely said to the storekeeper.

"Hello, children," said Mr. Brown. "How are you today?"

"Great!" said Reg. "Our birthday money came today!"

Keely came back clutching a tray of watercolors and two brushes. "Here they are, Reg," she said. "Wonderful colors: grass green, sky blue, sunshine yellow, strawberry red…I can make magic with these. I can't believe the day has finally come to take them home!"

"If you want to see magic, look through this," Reg said, holding the magnifying glass he had chosen. Keely held it in one hand and looked at her other hand.

"It's amazing, all right," she said. "My fingernails look huge. After my paints, this is the best thing in the store."

"Oh, lovely paints," said Mr. Brown. "I myself

am an artist. I love to paint. You must bring some of your work for me to see."

"I will," said Keely.

"And you have made a wonderful choice too," Mr. Brown said to Reg. "You will be able to see the smaller wonders of the world through that magnifying glass."

"I can hardly wait to start," Reg told him. "I have wanted one of these for a long time."

They paid Mr. Brown and started home. On the

way, they met their good friend Burt. Reg took out the magnifying glass to show him.

"Cool!" Burt exclaimed. "Look at the threads on my shirt! I can see the spaces between the threads and even the little hairs on the threads. I sure wish I had one of these."

"We can play with mine together," said Reg. "See you at the game after my music lesson."

When they got home, Reg was still talking about the magnifying glass. "It's just what I need to get a good look at rocks and grains of sand. I'm going to keep it safe in its box on my desk. It's my new favorite thing."

After lunch, Reg played with his magnifying glass so long that he was almost late for his music lesson. He left the house in a sprint. Soon after Reg left, Burt came by to pick up the catcher's mitt that Reg had forgotten to take for the game. "It's not like Reg to forget his mitt," he said to Keely, shaking his head. "I hope he can throw the ball straight."

Keely decided that her first painting would be of the flowers in the field by her house. She packed up her new paints and a pad of paper. Then she thought about how beautiful the flowers would look through Reg's magnifying glass. She took it off his desk and slipped it into her knapsack. "I'll just borrow it to see the flowers. I'll be extra careful," she said to herself.

When Keely got to the field, she took out the magnifying glass and looked at a bright yellow flower. She could see the tiny grains of pollen sticking to a honeybee's legs. She began to paint a picture of the flower up close, with the honeybee in the middle.

When the picture was almost finished, a butterfly flew past Keely's head. She thought about how wonderful it would be to see the butterfly through the magnifying glass. She ran after the butterfly. Every time she got near, the butterfly would flutter off. At last it landed on a bright blue flower and began to probe the center with its long tongue. Keely was very close when she tripped over a rock and fell. She felt a stinging pain in her knee and saw blood. Then she saw the magnifying glass on

the ground, its lens broken in two. Big tears came to Keely's eyes.

"Oh no! Look what I've done!" she cried. "Reg will be so mad at me. Everyone will be mad at me."

Keely picked up the broken magnifying glass and limped back to where she had been. She gathered up her painting and paints and stumbled home. When she got there, she hid the box in the back of her closet. I just can't tell him, she thought. He will never forgive me, ever.

When Reg got home from the ball game, he went straight to his desk. "Hey!" he shouted. "Where's my magnifying glass? I left it right here! Did you move it?" he asked his mother.

"No, dear," she said.

"Do you know where it is?" he asked Keely.

"Have you lost it already?" she asked him.

"I haven't done anything with it," he told her. "It just disappeared."

Keely looked at her feet. "Well, I've been busy with my paints," she said.

"Who could have taken it?" he said. He thought a minute. "Burt!" he said. "I sent him to get my catcher's mitt. Burt was in my room today, and he really liked that magnifying glass."

Keely looked up. She stared at her brother. "Burt would never ever take anything of yours," she said. "He's your best friend."

"I thought he was," said Reg. "I'm going right over to ask him if he took it."

"No, Reg!" Keely said. "You can't do that."

"Why not?" Reg asked.

"Well…" started Keely, "because…"

"Yes?" said Reg.

"Because he didn't take it. I'm sure."

"And how can you be sure?" asked Reg.

"I'm pretty sure the magnifying glass was on your desk after Burt left."

"There was no one else in the house, Keely. It had to be Burt! Don't bother trying to defend that thief."

Keely chewed her knuckles. "You're wrong, and I'm sure because…because it was…me," said Keely.

"I thought I could just borrow it and put it back and you would never know, but I fell down…" Keely showed Reg her bandaged knee.

"And my magnifying glass?" he asked.

Keely took the box from her closet and opened it. "I'm really, really sorry, Reg."

"How could you, Keely? It was brand-new and my favorite thing. What if I had talked to Burt about it? I feel terrible that I thought it was him."

"I feel terrible too," Keely said. "What can I do to make it up to you? I can give you something of mine." Keely sighed. "You can have my new paints. I will buy you another magnifying glass as soon as I can earn the money."

"I don't want your paints," said Reg. "I want my magnifying glass. You know how long I've wanted one."

"I know," said Keely. "The paints are almost new. Maybe Mr. Brown will take them back as a trade for a new magnifying glass."

"He won't," said Reg.

"Let's just try," Keely said. "I'll take my painting to show him how good the paints are."

"That's a very sad story," said Mr. Brown after Keely told him what had happened. "What you did was not good," he told Keely, "but I would hate to see an artist like you without paints. What can we do?"

He held his chin in his hand and thought. Then he said to Keely, "If you paint me a picture just like that one, but much bigger, on that wall over there, I will give you a new magnifying glass to give to your brother."

"Really?" said Reg.

"Really," said Mr. Brown. He turned to Keely. "It will be a lot of work. The wall will have to be cleaned first. Then you can use these special paints and these brushes."

"It's a deal!" said Keely. "I'll start tomorrow! Thank you very much, Mr. Brown."

"This is so great," said Keely as they walked home.

Reg gave her a look.

"I know what you're thinking," Keely said, "but I've learned my lesson. I double-triple promise for sure that I will never take anything of yours without asking again, ever."

"Okay then," said Reg. "I believe you." He punched Keely's arm lightly, and she punched him back.

"Now I'm going to find Burt," said Reg, "and tell him what a good friend I think he is."

"Good idea," said Keely.

The Hottest Day

Reg woke up on the first day of summer vacation. He threw off his covers. The sun was shining through the window. The day was already getting very warm. He went to wake up Keely.

"Wow, is it hot!" said Keely. "Now it feels like summer!"

At the breakfast table, their mother said, "Do you two remember that Grandma is coming for supper tonight?"

"Of course we remember," Reg said. "Today is Grandma's birthday. Her present is in my room. I wrapped it myself."

"I'm all ready too," said Keely.

Their mother smiled at them. "What are you going to do for fun on this very hot day?"

"We're meeting Burt and Shawna at Big Tree," said Reg.

Keely had peeled her banana and arranged the four strips to make a letter *K*. "*K* for Keely," she said. Then she sang,

> Keely, Keely, banana peely,
> Very hot is how I feely.

Reg rolled his eyes at Keely. "We'll decide together what we are going to do," he told his mother.

Keely and Reg headed off to Big Tree, and on the way Keely sang,

> Hot, hot, summer day,
> Too hot to run, too hot to play.

Reg joined in, and they sang it again and again.

When they got to Big Tree, they found Burt and Shawna sitting in the shade. Shawna was fanning herself with a big leaf.

"This is awful," Shawna said. "I've never been so hot."

Burt turned to his friends. "What do we want to do today?"

"It's too hot to play chase," said Reg.

"Or run races," said Shawna.

Burt said maybe they could just sleep, but everyone else said, "That's boring."

"I have an idea," said Keely. "I know the very best thing to do when it's hot."

"What?" the others asked all at once.

"Swim!" said Keely. "Swim in the river!"

"Yes!" said Shawna. "That's perfect. I could stay in the water all day."

"We have to find a grown-up to watch us," said Burt. "Let's ask my dad."

Burt and Reg and Shawna and Keely went to Burt's house to ask Burt's dad. He was sitting at his desk.

"Dad," said Burt, "will you watch us swim in the river?"

"That sounds wonderful," he told them. "I wish I could, but I have to take these papers to the office right now." He sighed. "Maybe this afternoon when I get back."

"My dad's away," said Shawna, "but maybe my mom can watch us."

Shawna and Keely and Burt and Reg walked to Shawna's house. Shawna's mother was feeding Shawna's baby sister.

"Mom, can you watch us swim?" Shawna asked.

"It's the perfect day for it," said Shawna's mother. "I would like to, but I have to help out at the mothers' and toddlers' playgroup."

"Ohhh," said Shawna. She sighed.

"Maybe this afternoon when we get back," said Shawna's mother.

"We can get our mom to come," said Keely. "She loves to swim. Let's go ask her."

They all went back to Keely and Reg's house.

"Can you watch us swim, Mom? Please?" asked Reg.

"I'd love to," she said, "but you remember this is Grandma's birthday, and she's coming to dinner. I'm making all her favorite foods. There's still a lot to do."

"Oh," said Keely, "I remember now. But it's so hot."

"I'm sorry, dears. Maybe you can find another grown-up to watch you."

"All the grown-ups are busy," said Keely. "Grown-ups are always busy."

Just then the letter carrier came by with the mail.

"Hi, Rudy," they called. "Would you like to join us for a swim in the river?"

"Boy, would I!" he said. "But I have to deliver this whole bag of mail before I can think of resting or cooling off."

The kids sat down to think. Burt started to snore.

"I have it!" Reg said. "I have the answer to our problems! We can help Mom with the work. Then she can come with us! Let's go ask if we can help."

Keely and Reg found their mother at the sink. "Mom," said Keely, "if we help with the work, you can come swimming with us, right?"

"What a lovely idea," said Keely's mother. She looked around the house.

"Someone can put up the streamers," she said, "and make a Happy Birthday sign. Someone can wash these greens for the salad. The floor could use a little sweep, and the cushions need plumping. And who would like to set the table?"

"I'll do the sign," said Reg. "My writing is very neat. And I'm good at climbing, so I can put up the streamers."

"I'll wash the greens," said Burt. "The cold water will feel so good."

"I'll do the table," said Shawna. "I like to make things pretty. Can I pick some flowers too?"

"Of course," said Keely's mother. "I guess that leaves you with the sweeping, Keely."

"I can handle it," said Keely. She picked up the broom and started sweeping the floor. As she swept she sang quietly,

> Keely's broom goes sweepy sweepy.
> Find a penny, keepy keepy.

In just a little while, everything was done. Keely's mother put on her pineapple-print bathing suit. They all headed off to the river.

And that's just where Grandma found them.

Award-winning author **Jo Ellen Bogart** has written many popular picturebooks and non-fiction books for children. She loves animals and has had many unusual pets over the years, including, at the moment, a frog that she got as a tadpole twenty-three years ago. She lives in Guelph, Ontario.